DOG IN CHARGE

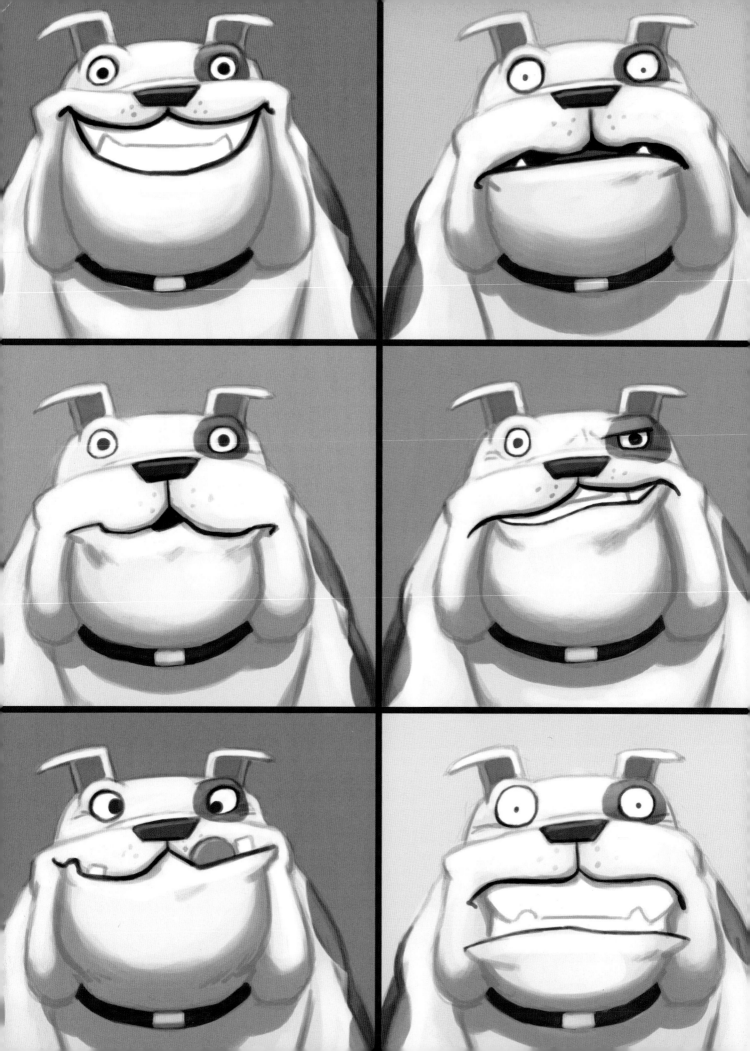

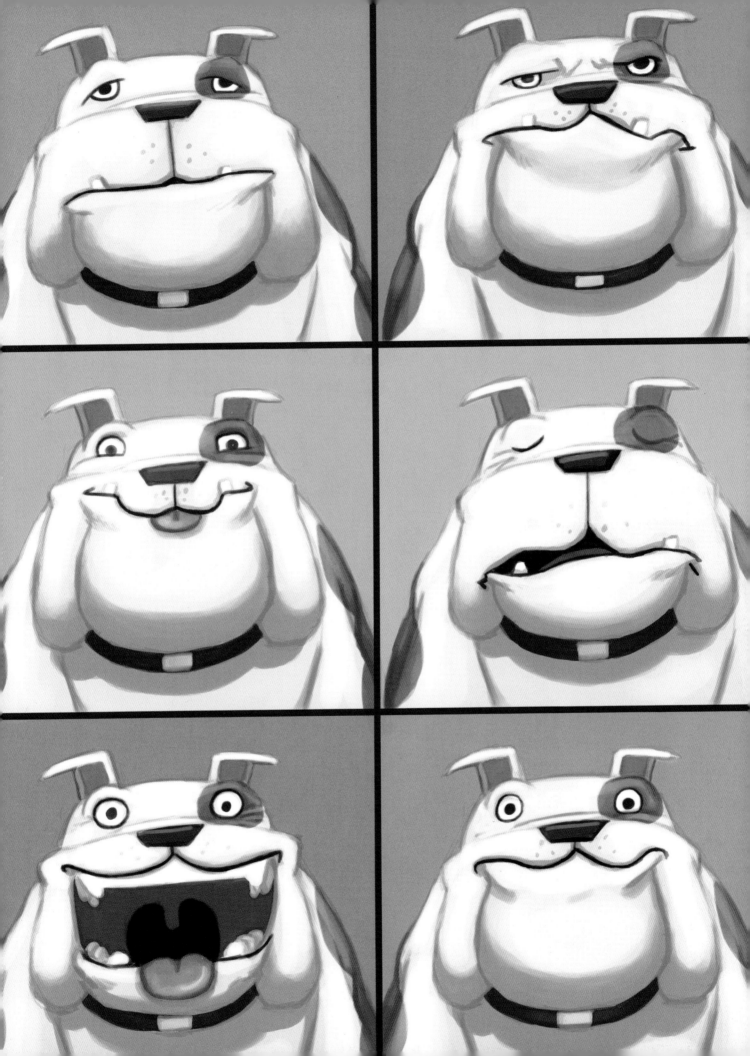

DOG IN CHARGE

by **K. L. GOING**   illustrated by **DAN SANTAT**

PUFFIN BOOKS

For Roxanne, the very best dog, and for my dad, who loved her.
—K.L.G.

For Leah, Alek, and Kyle.
—D.S.

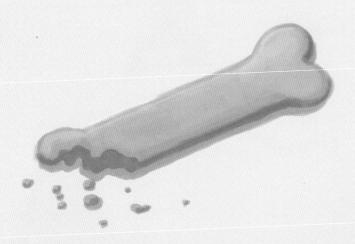

PUFFIN BOOKS
An imprint of Penguin Random House LLC
375 Hudson Street
New York, New York 10014

First published in the United States of America by Dial Books for Young Readers,
a division of Penguin Young Readers Group, 2012
Published by Puffin Books, an imprint of Penguin Random House LLC, 2016

THE LIBRARY OF CONGRESS HAS CATALOGED THE DIAL BOOKS FOR YOUNG READERS EDITION AS FOLLOWS:
Going, K. L. (Kelly L.)
Dog in charge / by K. L. Going ; pictures by Dan Santat.
p. cm.
Summary: When his human family goes to the store, Dog is left in charge of five wily cats.
ISBN 978-0-8037-3479-1 (hardcover)
1. Dogs—Juvenile fiction. 2. Cats—Juvenile fiction.
[1. Dogs—Fiction. 2. Cats—Fiction.] I. Santat, Dan, ill. II. Title.
PZ10.3.G562Do 2012
[E]—dc23
2011035211

Puffin Books ISBN 978-1-101-99773-4

Manufactured in China

1 3 5 7 9 10 8 6 4 2

Dog had a busy afternoon.

"Sit."

Dog sat.

"Stay."

Dog stayed.

"Dance."

Dog stood on his back paws and danced in a circle.

Then Dog got a scrumptious dog treat.

"Oh boy, oh boy, oh boy!"

thought Dog.

"Good Dog. Smart Dog. The very best Dog. We're going to the store, so now you will be in charge. Watch the cats, and make sure they don't get in any mischief."

The family bustled and hustled out the door,
into the car.

Dog watched them go,
eyeing the cats lined up in a row.

"First we will sit and then we will stay,"

thought Dog.

But the cats did not sit.

Where did all the cats go?

There were one, two, three, four, five

empty spots.

Dog looked in the kitchen.

"Down," barked Dog.

SPLASH! went the milk.

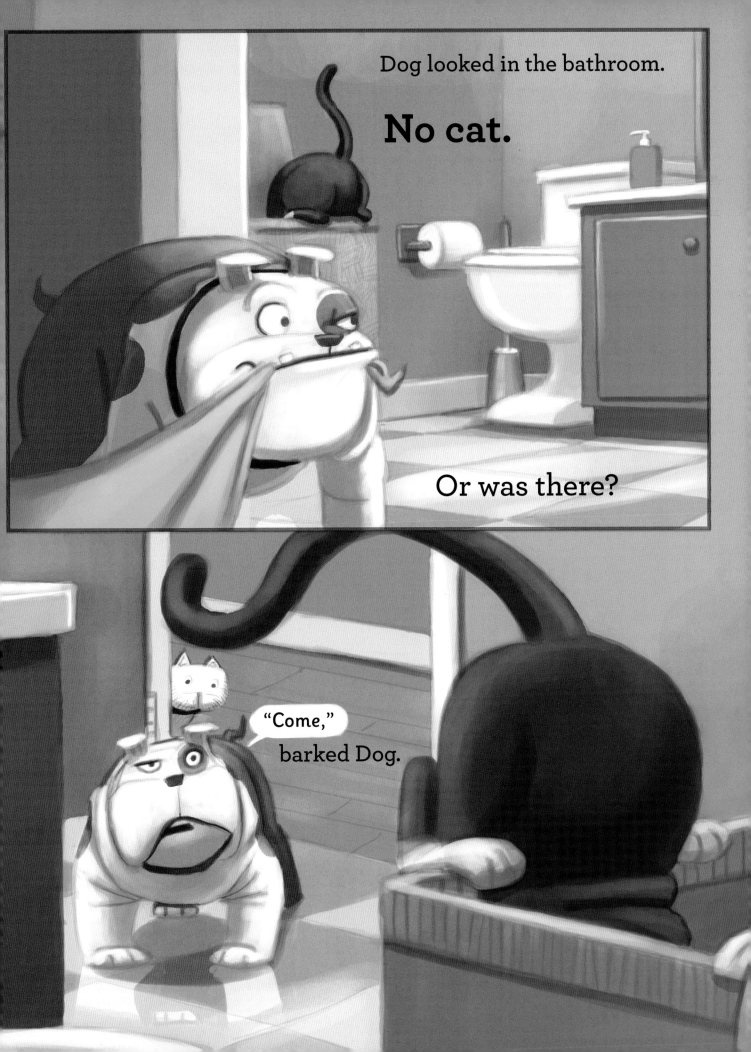

Soon the family would come home.
Would he still be a good Dog, a smart Dog, the very best Dog?
Would he get more scrumptious dog treats?

It was hard to be in charge.
Dog was hungry and tired.
He lay down to think.

Then Dog
had an idea.

Dog headed for
the kitchen.

Treats for
good cats!

GOOD KITTY
CAT TREATS

Dog's tummy rumbled.

Dog's nose twitched.

GOOD KITTY
CAT TREATS

Dog's mouth
opened.

Dog had to fix everything.
He tried to think, but his eyes
grew heavy and his paw was soft.

Then one, two, **three**, **four**, **five** little noses appeared.

PURR

went the cats.
They loved Dog.

So one, two, three, four, five cats
licked up the crumbs and milk.

One, two, three, four, five cats polished the living room.

One, two, three, four, five cats
neatened the bedroom.

One, two, three, four, five cats
straightened the bathroom.

Then one, two, **three,** **four, five** cats snuggled up next to Dog.

The sound of a car
rumbled in the driveway.

The
family
was home.

"Good Dog! Smart Dog! The very best Dog!"

Dog got lots of scrumptious dog treats.

"Were the cats good
while you were in charge?"

Dog barked.

He stood on his back legs and danced in a circle.

"Good cats,"

thought Dog.

"Smart cats.
  The very best cats."

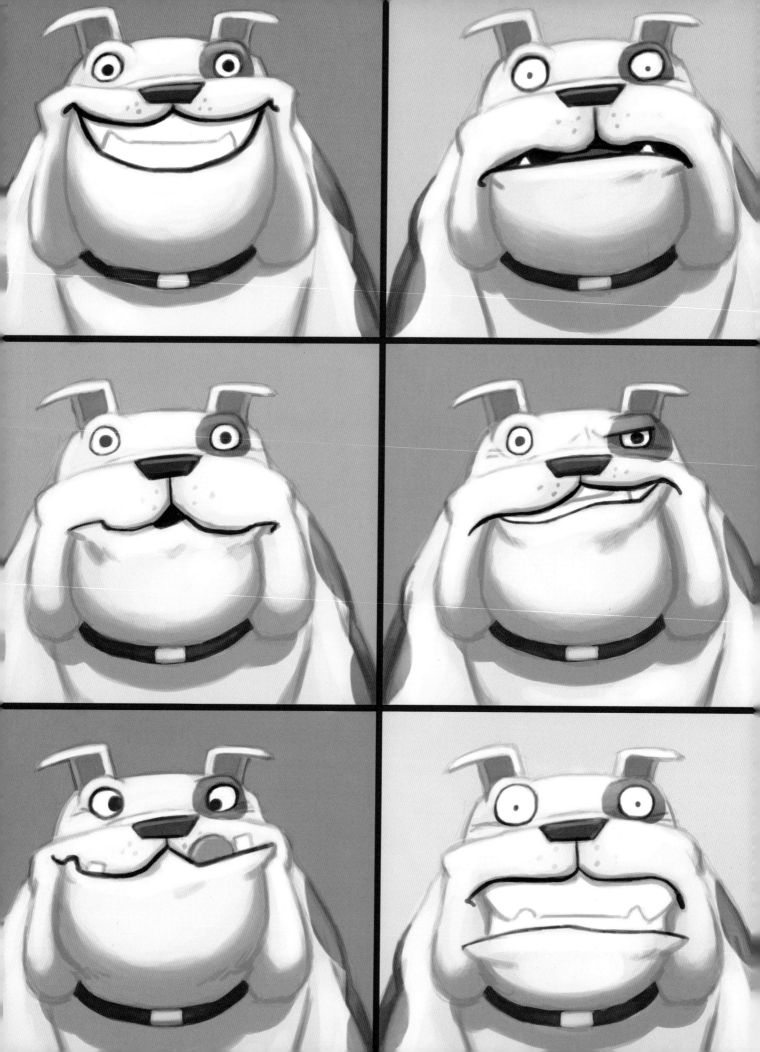

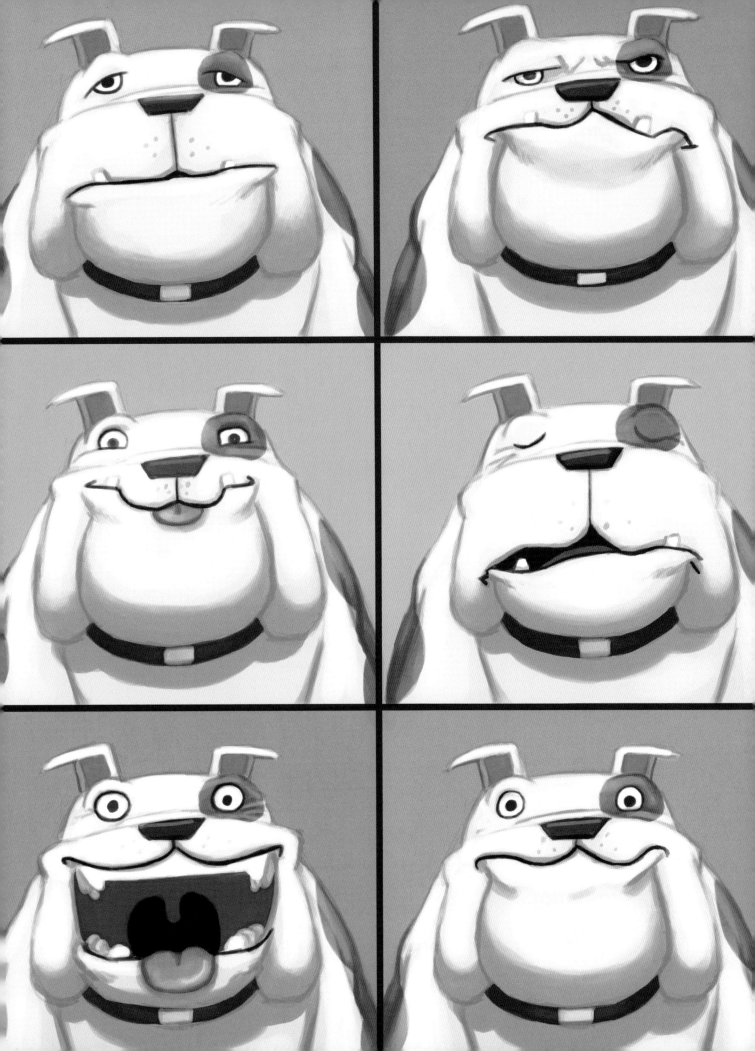